RIB TICKLING TALES OF
Akbar-Birbal

Compiled by
'KUNWAR' ANIL KUMAR

MANOJ PUBLICATIONS

CONTENTS

Manoj Publications

761, Main Road Burari, Delhi-110084
Phone : 27611116, 27611349
Fax : 27611546, Mobile : 9868112194
E-mail : manojpublications @ vsnl.net
Website : www.manojpublications.com
ISBN : 81-8133-407-8

Showroom :

1583-84, Dariba Kalan,
Chandani Chowk, Delhi-6
Phone : 23262174, 23268216
Mobile : 9818753569

Printers :
Jain Offset Printers

BIRBAL'S KHICHDI

ONE day, Birbal and Akbar were strolling in front of the palace. It was the afternoon time of a chilly winter season. Suddenly a Brahmin, in tattered clothes, came near them with folded hands.

"What do you want?" asked Akbar.

"Your Majesty! Please help me," the Brahmin requested with folded hands. "I am a very poor man. I get no good work to earn more. I spend the little money I earn, entirely on food. Now I am in need of one thousand gold coins for my daughter's marriage. We intend to give some ornaments to our only child—our daughter. Besides the ornaments, we will have to buy clothes and utensils. We must invite some people to take meals in our house, and so we will have to buy oil, flour, vegetables and spices."

"Look, when you have no money at all, why do you want to give ornaments to your daughter? When you cannot afford to buy good food for your own family, why do you dream of giving a party to other people?" asked the Emperor.

"It is my life-long ambition, Your Majesty!" said the Brahmin. "I am a poor father, but I too have a dream of spending some money for the marriage of my only child. I shall be extremely grateful to you, if you only give me an opportunity to earn the money, I now need so much for my daughter's marriage."

"Well, I give you an opportunity to earn one thousand gold coins," said the Emperor. "You go and stand in the cold water of the lake in this garden. You will come out of the water only after the sunrise, tomorrow."

Birbal grew anxious. He felt bad that the Emperor had become rather harsh with the poor Brahmin. He would not be able to stand in cold water for the whole night, and would definitely die.

But now the Brahmin looked happy. Accompanied by the guards, he went towards the lake and entered its cold water.

"The Brahmin will die of severe cold, sir!" said a guard to Birbal.

"I don't know," said Birbal. "Perhaps he is very strong in his mind. But the chances of his success are very slim."

But, next day, much to the happiness of them all, the Brahmin was alive and smiling. The sun had already risen. The Brahmin came out of the cold water of the lake—successful and victorious!

"How have you made an impossible task possible?" the Emperor asked. "It was a tough job. You have done a great feat! I just cannot believe it. Could you tell me your secret?"

"There is nothing secret about it, Your Majesty," said the Brahmin. "I was determined to achieve success."

"I asked you how you spent the night in cold water?" said Akbar.

"I kept looking at the lights of the palace."

"I see!" Akbar said. "So, you got all the warmth you needed from the lights of my palace and did not feel the chill of cold water and passed the night very comfortably. Well, in that case, I cannot give you any reward! You may go home!"

The Brahmin was shocked to hear this. How some lights at a distance of 100 yards send any warmth to a man standing in the cold water of the lake in a wintry night? Akbar just wanted an excuse. It was very unkind of him to have deprived the Brahmin of a promised sum.

Akbar turned his back and moved towards his palace.

The guards looked at one another's face helplessly. Birbal went back home, thinking deeply about the Brahmin.

Next day, Birbal went to the Emperor and said, "I have now learnt to cook khichdi. Please come to my residence tomorrow and have the taste of my special khichdi."

Akbar was pleased that Birbal had invited him to a lunch-party. Next day, Akbar reached Birbal's home. He was accompanied by his courtiers. Birbal welcomed them offering flowers while his servants sprinkled scented water on them. They were led to a big hall furnished with soft pillows and mattresses. Servants stood with giant hand fans.

Akbar was smiling all the time. He was pleased that Birbal looked to their comforts.

Two hours had passed and no one from Birbal's house had offered them even a glass of plain water. Akbar was hungry and thirsty too.

"Where is Birbal?" the Emperor asked.

"Outside, in the garden," replied the servant.

"When I asked you an hour ago, you gave me the same reply," said Akbar. "What is he doing there in the garden?"

"Excuse us, Your Majesty!" said the servant, "He is busy cooking khichdi."

Akbar became very angry. He stood up, shouting at the servants.

"Excuse us, Your Majesty!" said a servant, "We have told you just the truth. It is true that he is busy in the garden cooking khichdi!"

"Take us to him," ordered Akbar.

The servants led the Emperor and the courtiers into Birbal's garden. There Birbal was putting twigs and wood into the fire under a tall palm tree.

"Where is your khichdi?" asked Akbar.

Birbal stood up and quietly pointed his finger towards the top of the tree. A large pot was hanging from the top of the tall palm tree.

Akbar and all the courtiers craned their necks to see the pot.

"What is this?" Akbar was wild with rage! "We are hungry and you are showing us a big pot tied onto this tall tree?"

"I am sorry, Your Majesty!" said Birbal. "I think you will have to wait for some more time. I have put rice, pulses, and onions and garlic, all into the pot. Please see for yourself that I am putting a lot of firewood and twigs into the fire. But I do not know why it is taking so much time!"

"There is a gap of about ten yards between the pot and the fire," said Akbar. "How can the heat reach the pot hanging so high, up on the tree?"

"I think the heat from the fire on the ground is reaching the pot," said Birbal.

"You are talking absurd," shouted Akbar angrily.

"Excuse me, Your Majesty!" said Birbal. "If a poor Brahmin standing in the cold water can get warmth from the lights in the palace, burning at a distance of not less than 100 yards, this pot, too, can get the heat from the fire burning at a distance of ten yards only!"

"Now I get your point, Birbal," said the Emperor. "I should not have become cruel to that poor Brahmin. I am indeed very sorry. I promise to pay the Brahmin two thousand gold coins. Send him to me. I must thank you, for you have brought me to my senses."

Birbal was happy that the Brahmin would get his reward that had been doubled up to two thousand gold coins by the Emperor himself.

"Please come with me inside the house", said Birbal. "I have made arrangements for your meals. There are many tasty dishes and khichdi too."

They all laughed and followed Birbal into his house for the lunch.

❏ ❏

LIFE IS MOST DEAR

ONCE, Birbal and Emperor Akbar were chatting as usual. The Emperor said, "Birbal! What is it that is most dear to every person?" Birbal said, "Your Majesty, life is most dear to each and every living being."

"Can you prove it?" asked the Emperor.

"Yes, I can," replied Birbal.

After some days, Birbal brought a small baby of monkey along with its mother in the palace.

There was a large tank in the middle of the palace garden. Birbal ordered the servants to empty the tank. He told them to erect a long pole in the centre of the tank. Afterwards, he left the monkey and its baby in the tank and asked the servants to fill water in the tank slowly.

The Emperor watched all this with interest. As the water level began rising, the monkey climbed up higher on the pole with her baby clutching its body.

At last the water level rose so high that it reached the monkey's waist. The monkey lifted her baby up in her hands and stood up on the top of pole for safety.

The Emperor saw all this and exclaimed, "Look Birbal! How she is trying to save her baby! It means that her child is more dear to her than her own life!"

Meanwhile, the water level rose to her neck. The water started entering her nose and ears. It seemed as if she feared that she would drown.

The monkey looked around for a while and then placed her baby under her feet. She then stood upon her baby and started trying to come out of the water.

"Now see, Your Majesty! To save her own life, she did not care for her baby. She placed her baby under her feet and saved her own life. Doesn't this prove that one's life is most dear to everyone?"

The Emperor was shocked beyond words to comment. He simply said, "Birbal, what you say is true. Life is certainly most dear of all."

Birbal smiled and ordered the servants to bring down the water level in the tank and rescue the monkey and its baby.

❑ ❑

AKBAR was a great Emperor. He had several subsidiary Kings ruling under his power. Once, one such king thought of meeting Birbal. He wanted to know how clever he really was as he had heard a lot about him from other people.

Therefore, the King disguised himself as a farmer, sat on a horse and started for Delhi.

After reaching the outskirts of the city, the King came across a lame man, who was requesting the passers-by, "Sir, I am lame. I want to go to Delhi. Have pity on me. God will bless you if you kindly allow me to ride pillion on your horse."

The king felt sorry to see him in such a pitiable condition. He got down from his horse; helped the lame-man take his seat instead. When the lame man had sat properly on the horse, the King took the reins in his hand and started leading the horse on foot.

When they reached Delhi, the King said to the lame-man, "We've reached Delhi. Now please get down from the horse and go where you want."

The lame-man very surprisingly refused to get down. Instead he started shouting angrily, "How dare you! You seem to be a wicked person! I hired you to guide me upto Delhi. And now, you are asking me to get down from my horse?"

The king was astonished. He didn't know what to do.

Seeing him silent, the lame man shouted again, "Aren't you ashamed? You want to take advantage of my handicap and take away my horse!"

Once again, the King requested him to to get down from the horse and go away. But, instead, the lame man again started to shout at him. Both claimed the ownership of the horse. Finally, they went to the Emperor's court for justice.

The Emperor asked Birbal to solve the case.

Birbal listened to both of them carefully and asked a servant to tie the horse in the royal stable. Then he asked the lame man and the farmer to meet him the next day.

The next morning, when they arrived, Birbal took them to the stable. There were several horses in a row.

Birbal first asked the lame man to identify his horse. But the lame man failed to identify the horse and walked out of the stable.

Then, Birbal asked the King, in disguise of a farmer, to identify his horse. The king at once recognised his horse. The horse also neighed at the sight of his master.

He gave the horse back to the King and punished the lame man for cheating.

The king in disguise was extremely pleased to see Birbal's intelligence. He disclosed his real identity and told Emperor Akbar that he had come all the way to test the intelligence of Birbal. He said, "I am really impressed by his intelligence and presence of mind. He really is a gem."

Emperor Akbar became very happy and received the king with due honour.

THE REAL SLAVE

A rich man had a slave. One day, the slave robbed his master's house and absconded.

But, a few days later, when the master was going somewhere, he spotted his slave in a crowded market. The slave also saw his master. But there was no way for him to escape. Before the master could take any action, the slave held his master firmly by his arms and said, "You scoundrel! I have found you. Where were you running? I have spent a large amount on you."

At first, the master was stunned. But then, suppressing his anger, he said, "Cunning rascal! you think I am your servant? Return to your household duties, otherwise, I will thrash you badly." A big quarrel started between them on the street. Finally, they were taken to Birbal to solve the dispute.

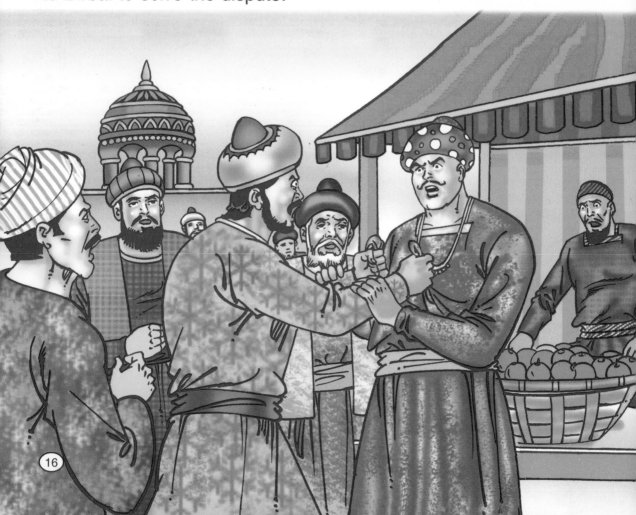

The master narrated Birbal the entire matter, "Sir, I had bought him for a large amount but now, he says that I am his slave!" Both of them said the same thing about each other.

Birbal then said to a guard, "Take them to a window and make them stick their heads out of it."

The guard obeyed Birbal. Then, Birbal told another guard, "Take a sword and cut off the slave's head!"

But before the guard could strike at the neck of one of them with his sword, the real slave quickly retracted his head in panic! It was exactly what Birbal had expected! He ordered the slave to go back to his master and work for him.

Everyone praised Birbal's intelligence and cleverness.

THE EMPEROR AND THE HOLY BOOK

ONE day, the Emperor said to Birbal, "Birbal, In your holy-book, it is written somewhere that, once Lord Vishnu ran all alone, hearing the cries of an elephant. He didn't even take his servants along with him. Why is it so? Weren't there any servants?"

Birbal said, "Maharaj, I shall answer your question at the right moment!"

Several days later, Birbal called the servant whose duty was to take the Emperor's grandson for a stroll everyday. Birbal gave him a statue of the Emperor's grandson made of wax.

He said to the servant, "Today when you take the Emperor's grandson for a walk, you take this statue also with you. Then pretend to have slipped near the tank in the garden. But, you should fall in such a manner that this statue is thrown into the water. Your successful performance will fetch you a handsome reward!"

The servant did as Birbal had asked him to do. As soon as he came near the tank, he, knowingly slipped and fell down throwing the statue into the tank.

The Emperor saw this happening from his balcony. He at once rushed to the spot and jumped into the tank with his clothes on. But he found the statue of his grandson in the water and realised his mistake.

Birbal was standing near the tank. He said, "Maharaj, Why did you yourself rush to the tank to save your grandson? Didn't you have servants? Why didn't you bring your servants with you?"

Birbal further said, "Your Majesty, just as your grandson is dear to you, so are the devotees of Lord Vishnu to him. That's the reason why on hearing the cries of the elephant for help, he himself ran to save him."

BIRBAL'S ILLNESS

ONCE, Birbal fell ill and didn't attend the court for many days. The Emperor got anxious and thought of visiting Birbal.

So, one day he went to Birbal's place. Birbal was very happy to see the Emperor.

Birbal had become very weak owing to fever. The Emperor wanted to know if Birbal's illness had affected his mental capacities. So, when Birbal went to another room to have some water, the Emperor stealthily placed four pieces of paper under the four legs of his bed.

When Birbal returned and lay on the bed, he noticed that there was some change in the room. He looked around to find out what it was.

Meanwhile, the Emperor kept chatting with him on purpose but Birbal was finding it difficult to be attentive.

Finally, the Emperor asked Birbal the cause of his diverted attention. Birbal replied, "I realise that some change has taken place in this bed."

"What change?" the Emperor asked with surprise.

"It appears as if the bed has sunk to a thickness of a paper or has risen otherwise!"

The Emperor understood that Birbal's illness had not at all affected his brain.

But still, acting as if he had understood nothing, the Emperor said, "One often feels like that during illness."

Birbal said, "Maharaj! Though I am physically ill, I am mentally all right."

The Emperor smiled and told him what he had done.

❏❏

THE DOG'S ROTI

ONE day, the Emperor and Birbal while taking a walk reached a small village.

In the way, the Emperor saw a dog who was eating a stale, black and dried piece of roti.

The Emperor thought of teasing Birbal. He said, "Look Birbal! that dog is eating 'Kali'."

Birbal understood what the Emperor meant. He replied, "Maharaj, It is 'Niyamat' for him!"

The Emperor lost his temper. He shouted, "Birbal, Don't you know, my mother's name is 'Niyamat' and you say that the dog is eating 'Niyamat'."

Birbal replied politely, "Maharaj, first, you gave 'Kali' to the dog to eat. You know very well that my mother's name is 'Kali'."

But the Emperor interrupted, "I didn't utter your mother's name. The roti was stale and had turned black."

Birbal replied, "But I also did not take your words seriously, Maharaj. I said that however stale and black the roti may be, it is 'Niyamat', that is, 'delight' for that hungry dog. I didn't mean to insult your mother!"

The Emperor kept quiet.

A STRAW IN THE THIEF'S BEARD

ONE day, the Emperor thought of an idea and decided to befool Birbal. He gave his ring to one of the courtiers and asked him to keep quiet. When Birbal came to the court, the Emperor said to him, "Birbal, today while taking bath I lost my ring! But I am sure that one of the courtiers must have stolen it. I know you are a good astrologer. Now, it is your responsibility to you find the thief. My ring is very precious."

Birbal said, "Where had you kept the ring before going for the bath?" The Emperor pointed towards a cupboard. Birbal went near the cupboard and placed his ear close to it as if he was trying to hear something. After some time, he said, "The cupboard has informed me that there is a small straw in the beard of the person who has stolen the ring."

When the courtier who had the ring in his possession heard Birbal, he touched his beard to examine it.

Birbal saw the courtier examining his beard and at once took him before the Emperor and said, "Maharaj this is the thief!" The Emperor was very pleased with Birbal and gave him a handsome reward.

THE BAG OF COINS

ONCE, there was a big quarrel between an oil seller and a butcher, and unable to settle their dispute, they went to Birbal.

When Birbal asked the butcher the reason behind the quarrel, he said, "I was selling meat in my shop when this oil seller approached me and asked me to bring the oil-container. But, when I had gone inside to fetch it, he took my bag full of money and began claiming that it was his bag.

But the oil-seller said, "No, sir, this is not true. The bag is really mine. In fact when I was taking out coins from the bag, he saw the money and began claiming that it was his. I want justice, Sir."

Birbal repeatedly asked them to come out with the truth but both of them insisted on their statement.

Finally, Birbal hit upon a solution to the tricky problem and poured water in a vessel and dipped all the coins from the bag in it. At once, a thin film of oil started floating upon the water surface; it clearly meant that the bag belonged to the oil-seller. So, Birbal returned the bag of coins to the oil-seller and punished the butcher.

❑❑

THE WAIL OF THE RIVER

IN was rainy season. Yamuna river was running in spate and overflowing. The gushing water was making a loud noise. The Emperor's palace was situated on the river bank. He was fast asleep.

It was a peaceful night and so, the frightening sound of the roaring river could be heard very clearly.

Suddenly in the midnight, the Emperor woke up because of the loud roaring sound of the river. He tried again to go back to sleep but the sound of the swirling water was so frightening and loud that he could not go to sleep again.

Finally, he got up and went near the window. Hearing the gushing water, the Emperor thought,—'could it be that the river was wailing?' He thought for a long time but he could not come to any conclusion.

The next morning, when the Emperor came to the court, he asked the courtiers, "Why is the river wailing?" But no one could give a satisfactory answer to it. Then the Emperor sent for Birbal.

When Birbal came, Emperor Akbar asked him the same question. Birbal said, "Your Majesty, I shall be able to answer your question only after listening to the river with my own ears."

The Emperor agreed, "Well, then tonight, you be in my palace!"

In the night, it was calm and quiet everywhere and the river could be heard weeping. Birbal was with the Emperor in his palace.

Again, the Emperor posed the same question before Birbal. Birbal said, "Your Majesty, the river is going to her husband's (the sea's place) from her father (mountain). She is feeling very sad to leave her father's house and so, she is wailing."

The Emperor and other courtiers were very pleased with Birbal's reply.

❏❏

THE DONKEY AND THE EMPEROR

ONE day, Emperor Akbar and Birbal went together for a walk. At the sunset Birbal sat down on the river-bank and performed 'sandhya'— the Hindu ritual. The Emperor was very much impressed. He said to Birbal, "Birbal, tell me how to perform 'sandhya'. I like it very much and I too like to do it."

Birbal replied, "Your Majesty, only Brahmins are supposed to perform 'sandhya' and not others."

"Then, make me a Brahmin," Emperor Akbar said.

Birbal replied, "No Maharaj, it is not possible!" But the Emperor insisted, "Why not? For me, everything is possible!"

Birbal was in a fix. He said, "Please give me some time for this."

The Emperor agreed. But after a few days, he again reminded Birbal of his promise. Then Birbal called a potter and said to him, "Tomorrow evening, you come to the riverside with your donkey and bathe him by scrubbing him vigorously. The Emperor and I will come there at that time. When we ask, 'What are you doing?' You would say, 'I am changing this donkey into a horse!' "

Accordingly, the next day, the potter came to the river bank with his donkey. He started bathing and scrubbing the animal. The Emperor who happened to notice this strange sight asked the potter, "What are you doing?"

"Maharaj, I am changing my donkey into a horse," said the potter politely. The Emperor roared into laughter. He said to Birbal, "This man appears to be mad. Can anyone change a donkey into a horse?"

Birbal said, "Your Majesty, if one cannot change a donkey into a horse, how is it possible to convert a Muslim into a Brahmin?"

The Emperor was convinced and said, "Birbal, you are right!"

A DOG AND A SON-IN-LAW

ONE day, Emperor Akbar said to Birbal, "Birbal! Bring me two such animals—one of which has a sense of gratitude and the other who forgets all this and takes to treachery."

After thinking deeply over the matter, Birbal brought a dog and his own son-in-law to the court.

He presented them before the Emperor, and said, "Maharaj, I have brought these two as per your wish!"

The Emperor asked, "Birbal, now explain who is faithful and who is treacherous?"

Birbal replied, "Jahanpanah, this dog eats only leftovers and yet remains faithful to his master. Even if he is beaten or driven out of the house, he remains loyal to his master and comes to him at once when called back.

But, on the contrary, a son-in-law is a very ungrateful person. Even if you give him everything, he is never satisfied. The more you give him, the more he wants. He only thinks about his own interest. Even if his father-in-law has to take to begging on the streets!"

The Emperor was very pleased with Birbal's answer and asked the guards to hang Birbal's son-in-law to death. Then, he ordered them to give enough milk to the dog.

Birbal was taken aback to hear the Emperor's orders. He said, "Jahanpanah! But I did not mean that only my own son-in-law is an ungrateful person. I referred to all the sons-in-law in the world. Therefore, it would be unfair to punish only my son-in-law. You too are someone's son-in-law."

The Emperor realised his mistake and withdrew his orders.

❏❏

AN ANGEL AND A WITCH

ONE day, the Emperor expressed his desire to see an angel and an ugly witch. He expressed his wish to Birbal.

The next day, Birbal came to the court along with his wife and a prostitute. Then presenting his wife he said to the Emperor, "Maharaj, this is an angel. I get endless satisfaction and happiness from her."

The Emperor looked at Birbal's wife and said, "Birbal, but the angels are said to be very beautiful. She is dark and weak. In the Puranas, angels have been described as stunning beauties."

Then Birbal said, "Maharaj! True beauty lies in the quality of an individual, not in the colour of the skin. She is an angel for me."

Birbal, now brought the prostitute before the Emperor. The Emperor saw her and exclaimed, "Wow! She is such a beauty! Look at her beautiful clothes and expensive ornaments." Upon which Birbal said, "All these are just to flatter the world. He who comes under her evil shadow, surely destroys his own life." The Emperor understood Birbal and realized that character and quality of a person determine his or her beauty.

THE SINGING FAKIR

ONCE an unknown fakir (saint) came wandering to the Emperor's palace and sat on the parapet. He was praying and singing. Hours passed, but he showed no signs of leaving the place. The servants asked him to leave the palace but he did not listen to them. Since he was a fakir, it was not possible to apply force to drive him out of the palace. The servants were thinking of how to get rid of him. In the meantime, the Emperor arrived in the palace and politely requested the fakir, "Oh holy sir! This is a palace and not a dharamshala. You are mistaken if you think that you can sit anywhere you think suitable and start meditating."

The fakir looked at the Emperor and asked coolly, "Your Majesty, who occupied this palace before you?"

"First it was my grand father," Emperor Akbar replied. "Afterwards my father occupied this palace and now I live here. And after me, by God's grace, my sons, and my grand sons too will stay here."

"Hmm, so!" the fakir exclaimed. "This means one person comes and the other goes. Then isn't this a dharamshala? This world too is like a dharamshala. We all are like guests. We stay here for a while and then go away. After that other people arrive in this world to stay. So, it is quite meaningless to say that this is my house and that is yours! You are foolish indeed to boast that this is your palace!"

The Emperor was speechless with the fakir's explanation. The fakir was really very knowledgeable. Just then the fakir removed his false beard and disguise. In fact, it was Birbal in the guise of a fakir. The Emperor was very pleased with Birbal and praised him open heartedly.

❏❏

DARK BELOW THE LAMP

ONCE, the Emperor and Birbal were sitting in the palace balcony and watching the sunrise. The sunrays falling on the sparkling waters of the Yamuna river gave it a golden sheen. The Emperor used to watch this natural beauty everyday.

Suddenly, their attention was diverted due to a loud noise. They noticed some thieves running after looting some travellers. The poor travellers were crying in grief.

The Emperor ordered his guards to catch the thieves but the thieves had already disappeared. The guards returned empty handed.

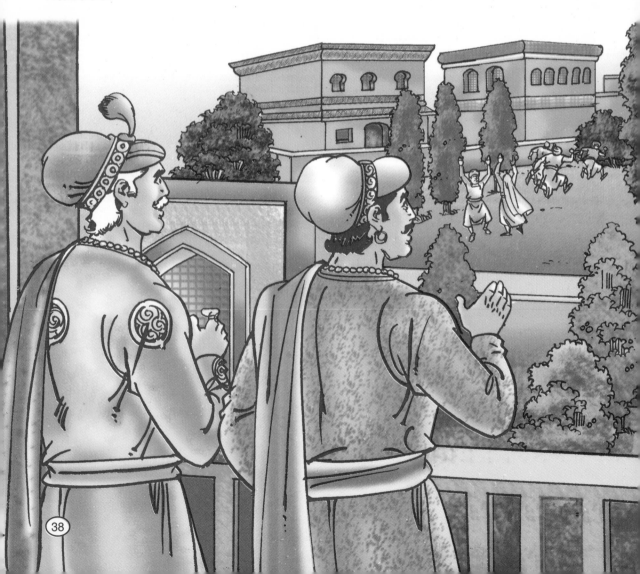

The Emperor was furious to see the soldiers coming back empty handed. Nothing could have been worse than the incapability of the royal guards in capturing the thieves who had robbed the passers-by near the palace itself.

The Emperor was terribly frustrated at this. He asked Birbal, "Birbal, all this has happened because our administration is not efficient. Isn't it a matter of shame? A common man is being robbed in front of the Emperor and the Emperor is incapable of doing anything in this regard; why is it so?"

Birbal said, "Your Majesty, though a lamp spreads light all around, but it is always dark under the lamp."

The Emperor was very much pleased with Birbal's reply. He compensated the travellers by giving them money and clothes etc. He also sent armed guards to escort them to their homes safely.

"DAULAT"

ONE day Daulat, a slave, who worked at Emperor Akbar's court, made some mistake and incurred his wrath. Emperor Akbar asked him to leave the court.

He went to Birbal's house. Birbal listened to him and suggested, "Once again, you go to the court and ask the Emperor, "Daulat has come, should he stay or leave?"

The Emperor was surprised to see him back. Daulat said to him, "Forgive me, Your Majesty. Should 'Daulat' stay or go away?". The Emperor was pleased with the double meaning of 'Daulat' (riches). He said, "Let it stay!"

None with a balanced state of mind would say, "Let 'Daulat' (riches) go away?"

"Tell me," the Emperor asked him, "who gave you, this idea?"

Daulat said, "It was Birbalji, Sir!"